SIDNEY MEMORIAL PUBLIC LIBRARY

0 00 03 0189789 8

C0-EDY-791

```
SIDNEY J 796.332 BUCK
Buckley, James,
Von Miller and the Denver
Broncos :
```

NOV 29 2016

SIDNEY MEMORIAL PUBLIC LIBRARY
8 River Street
Sidney, NY 13838
607-563-1200
www.sidneylibrary.org

VON MILLER
and the
Denver Broncos

SUPER BOWL 50

By James Buckley Jr.

Consultant: Craig Ellenport
Former Senior Editor, NFL.com

BEARPORT
PUBLISHING

New York, New York

Credits
Cover and Title Page, © Kevin Terrell via AP; 4, © Chris Williams/Icon Sportswire/Newscom; 5, © AP Photo/Gregory Payan; 6, © Rich Graessle/Icon Sportswire CGV/Newscom; 7, Courtesy DeSoto High School; 8, © Patrick Green/Icon SMI BAD/Newscom; 9, © Anthony Vassar/Zuma Press/Newscom; 10, © AP Photo/Darron Cummings; 11, © Zach Bollinger/Icon SMI DAL/Newscom; 12, © David J. Phillip/AP Photo; 13, © Erik William/Cal Sport Media/Newscom; 14, © Hector Acevedo/Zuma Press/Newscom; 15, © Robin Alam/Icons Sportswire164; 16, © AP Photo/Chris Carlson; 17, © Gary C. Caskey/UPI; 18, © Tony Avelar/EPA/Newscom; 19, © Rich Graessle/Icon Sportswire CGV/Newscom; 20, © Kevin Dietsch/UPI/Newscom; 21, © Anthony Behar/Sipa USA/Newscom; 22L, © Khaled Sayed/UPI/Newscom; 22R, © Chris Williams/Icon Sportswire/Newscom; 22 (Background), © Brian Kersey/UPI/Newscom.

Publisher: Kenn Goin
Editor: Jessica Rudolph
Creative Director: Spencer Brinker
Photo Research: Shoreline Publishing Group LLC

Library of Congress Cataloging-in-Publication Data

Names: Buckley, James, Jr., 1963- author.
Title: Von Miller and the Denver Broncos : Super Bowl 50 / by James Buckley, Jr. ; consultant: Craig Ellenport, former senior editor, NFL.com.
Description: New York : Bearport Publishing Company, Inc., (2017) | Series: Super Bowl Superstars | Includes bibliographical references, webography and index.
Identifiers: LCCN 2016019975 (print) | LCCN 2016025608 (ebook) | ISBN 9781944102968 (library binding) | ISBN 9781944997427 (ebook)
Subjects: LCSH: Miller, Von, 1989—Juvenile literature. | Football players--Biography—Juvenile literature. | Denver Broncos (Football team)—History—Juvenile literature. | Super Bowl (50th : 2016 : Santa Clara, Calif.)
Classification: LCC GV939.M52 B83 2017 (print) | LCC GV939.M52 (ebook) | DDC 796.33092 (B) --dc23

LC record available at https://lccn.loc.gov/2016019975

Copyright © 2017 Bearport Publishing Company, Inc. All rights reserved. No part of this publication may be reproduced in whole or in part, stored in any retrieval system, or transmitted in any form or by any means, electronic, mechanical, photocopying, recording, or otherwise, without written permission from the publisher.

For more information, write to Bearport Publishing Company, Inc., 45 West 21st Street, Suite 3B, New York, New York 10010. Printed in the United States of America.

10 9 8 7 6 5 4 3 2 1

Contents

Tackling Superman..................4
Young Von..........................6
Working Hard.......................8
A Great Start.....................10
A Tough Season....................12
Help from a Teammate..............14
A Big Win.........................16
Touchdown!........................18
Super Bowl MVP....................20

Key Players.......................22
Glossary..........................23
Bibliography......................24
Read More.........................24
Learn More Online.................24
Index.............................24

Tackling Superman

It was February 2016. **Linebacker** Von Miller and his Denver Broncos teammates were about to play the Carolina Panthers in Super Bowl 50. The Broncos had the best **defense** in the **NFL**, but the Panthers had the highest-scoring **offense**. Panthers **quarterback** Cam "Superman" Newton was strong, fast, and great at avoiding tacklers.

As the game began, Von focused on Newton. Would the young linebacker be able to tackle Superman?

Cam Newton throws a pass just before getting tackled during the Super Bowl.

Von Miller (#58) runs toward Carolina quarterback Cam Newton during Super Bowl 50.

Super Bowl 50 was played in Santa Clara, California, on February 7, 2016.

Young Von

Vonnie B'Vsean Miller Jr. grew up in DeSoto, Texas. As a kid, Von was often teased because he wore thick glasses. In the fifth grade, he joined a peewee football team, and the teasing soon stopped. Why? Von showed his teammates that he could play very well even while wearing glasses.

When he got older, Von played defense on his high school's football team. He was so good at tackling that opponents often ran plays as far away from Von as possible! After high school, many colleges asked him to join their football teams. In 2007, Von chose to attend Texas A&M University.

Today, Von wears glasses off the field but uses contacts when he's playing football.

At DeSoto High School, Von played on the Eagles football team.

Three of Von's teammates from peewee football also grew up to play in the NFL. Damontre Moore plays for the Raiders, Tony Jerod-Eddie plays for the 49ers, and Cyrus Gray plays for the Broncos.

Working Hard

The coaches at Texas A&M knew Von could one day be an amazing player. However, he sometimes skipped classes, and he didn't work hard in football practice. In spring of his first year, he was **suspended** from the team.

Von learned his lesson. He didn't want to waste an opportunity to play the game he loved. When he rejoined the team, he worked harder than ever. In 2009, his third season, he led the nation's college football players with 17 **sacks**!

Von with a Texas A&M teammate

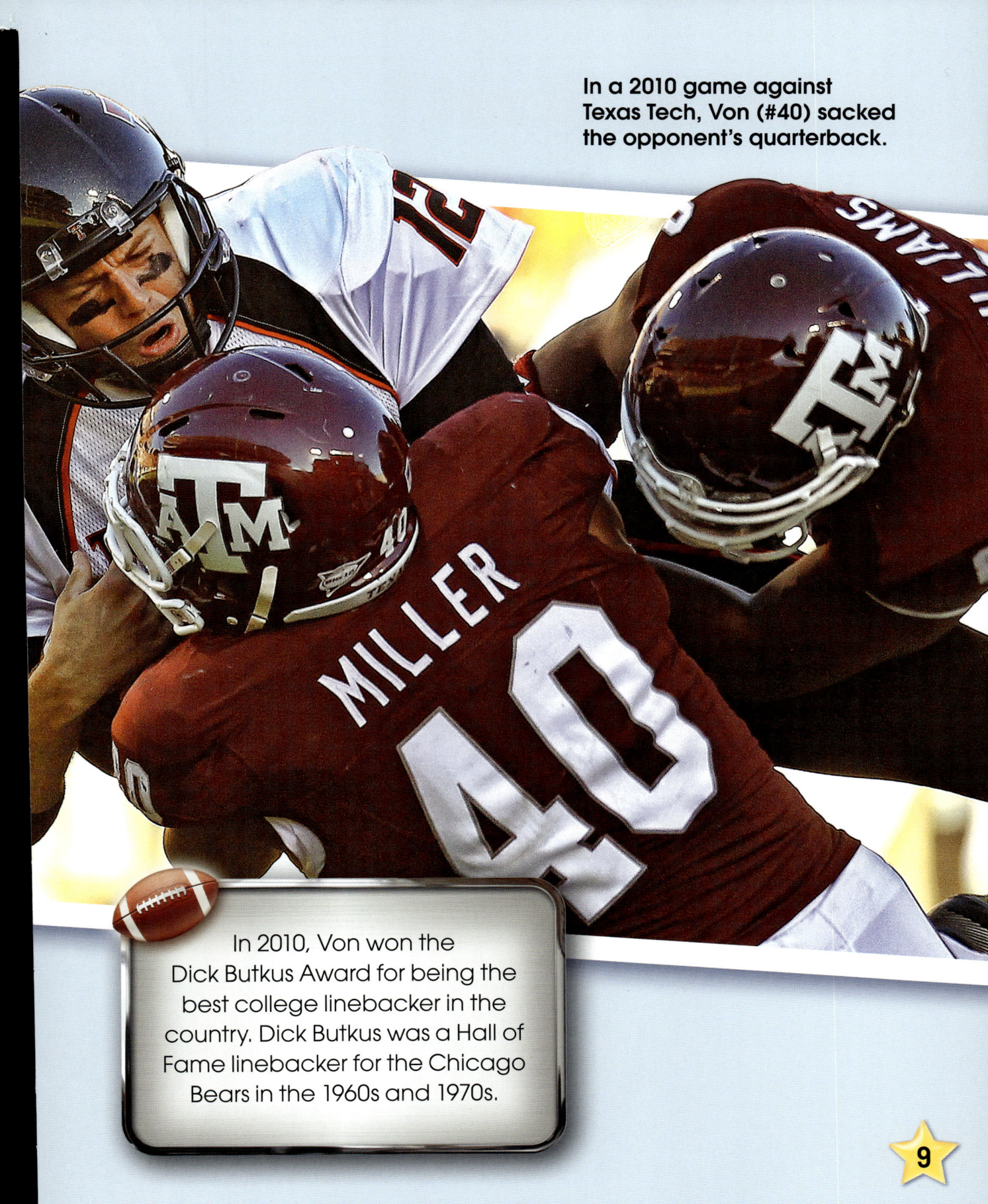

In a 2010 game against Texas Tech, Von (#40) sacked the opponent's quarterback.

In 2010, Von won the Dick Butkus Award for being the best college linebacker in the country. Dick Butkus was a Hall of Fame linebacker for the Chicago Bears in the 1960s and 1970s.

A Great Start

In 2011, the Denver Broncos chose Von as the second pick in the NFL **draft**. Von had a great first year. He made 64 tackles and 11.5 sacks, and he was named the Defensive **Rookie** of the Year.

Von's second season was even better. He made 18.5 sacks and forced 6 **fumbles**. He also returned an **interception**, speeding down the field for his very first NFL touchdown! After the 2012 season, Von was named to the league's all-star team.

Von with his Defensive Rookie of the Year trophy

Von (#58) teams with Chris Harris Jr. to sack Indianapolis Colts quarterback Andrew Luck.

How does a player earn half (0.5) a sack? When two teammates tackle a quarterback at the same time, each gets credit for half the sack.

A Tough Season

After a great 2012 season, Von's third season did not start well. In the summer of 2013, he broke NFL rules about being tested for drugs. The league suspended Von for Denver's first six games. He returned to the team in October, but two months later, he injured his right knee while making a tackle. He had to sit out the rest of the season so he could heal.

Even without Von, Denver made it to Super Bowl XLVIII (48). However, the Broncos were defeated by the Seattle Seahawks, 43–8. Von was sad, knowing he could have helped his team win the game.

After his knee was injured, Von was able to walk off the field with the team doctor.

Von lines up before a play starts during a December 2013 game against the Houston Texans.

The NFL regularly tests players to make sure they're not taking drugs that give them an unfair advantage.

13

Help from a Teammate

By the start of the 2014 season, Von had recovered from his injury. A new teammate helped him become a better player, too. DeMarcus Ware, who had been playing in the NFL for nine years, joined the Broncos. He became a **mentor** to Von. "Success is not just in one person," Ware told Von. "It's a team deal." Von learned that he needed to follow all the rules and work hard to support his team.

Before games, Von often signs autographs for fans.

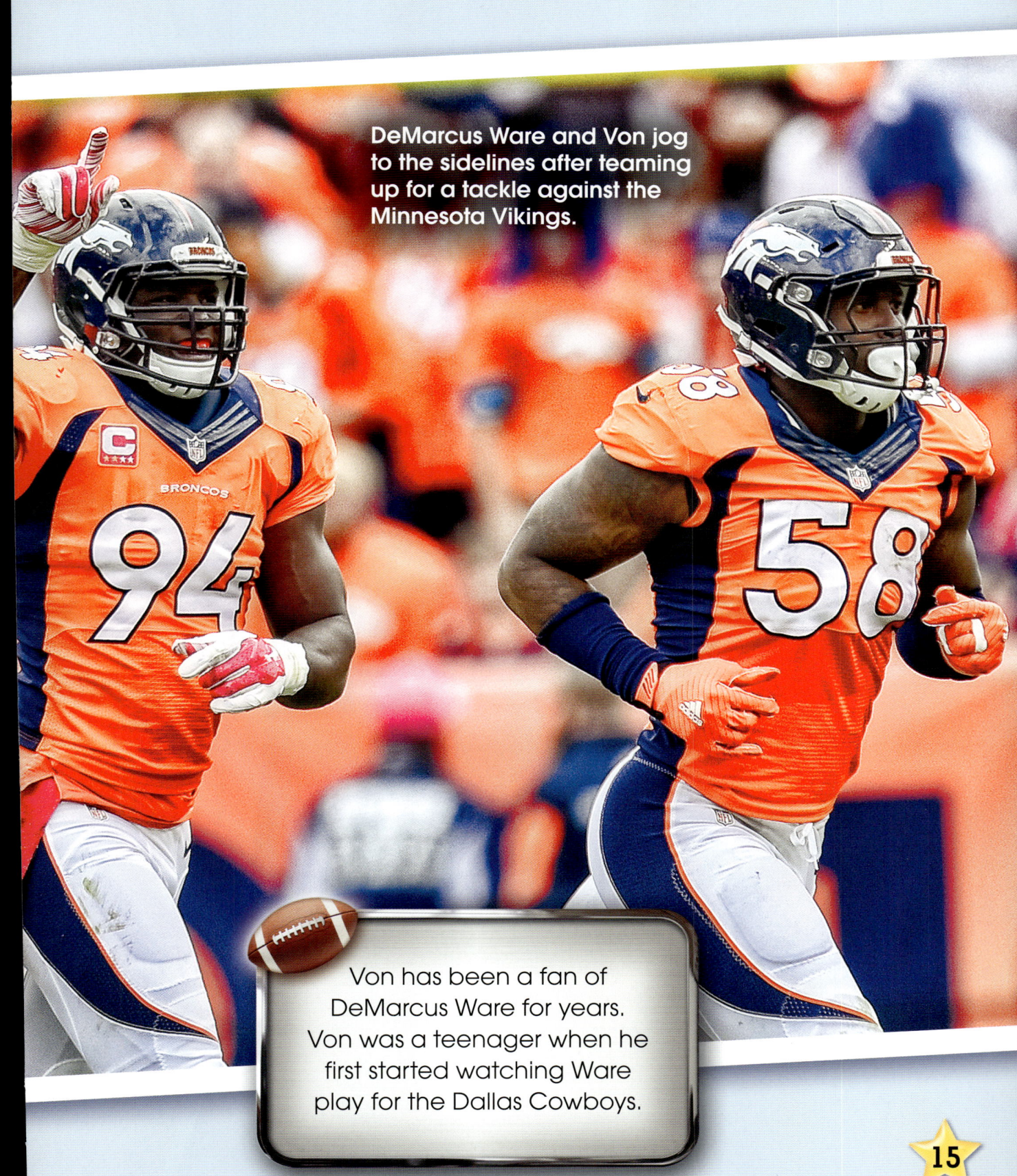

DeMarcus Ware and Von jog to the sidelines after teaming up for a tackle against the Minnesota Vikings.

Von has been a fan of DeMarcus Ware for years. Von was a teenager when he first started watching Ware play for the Dallas Cowboys.

A Big Win

In 2015, the Broncos finished the season 12–4 and made the **playoffs**. They faced the New England Patriots and their **legendary** quarterback, Tom Brady, in the **AFC Championship Game.** During key plays, Von fought his way through the offense and sacked Brady 2.5 times. The linebacker also made five tackles and an interception.

Denver won the game in a close 20–18 victory. The Broncos were going back to the Super Bowl. This time, Von was healthy and had a never-give-up attitude!

Von makes an interception during the AFC Championship Game.

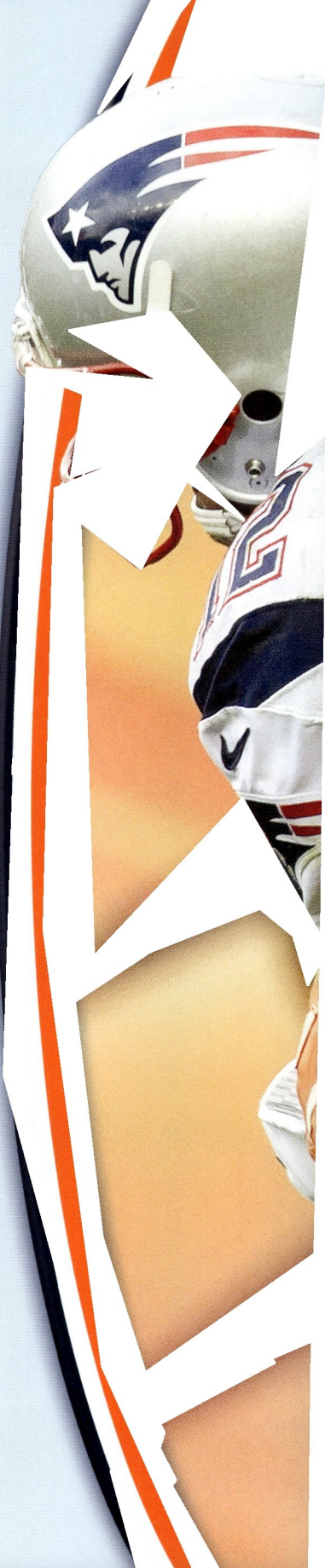

Von sacking Tom Brady

The Broncos have played in eight Super Bowl games. That number ties them with the Cowboys, the Patriots, and the Steelers for the most Super Bowl appearances.

Touchdown!

In Super Bowl 50, Von made the biggest play of the game during the first quarter. First, he sped past a Carolina blocker. Then he smashed into Cam Newton and grabbed the football from the quarterback. The ball fell from Von's hands, and Denver's Malik Jackson fell on the fumble in the **end zone**. Von had sacked Superman, and it led to a touchdown for Denver!

Von kept up the pressure on Newton and sacked him 1.5 more times. By the fourth quarter, the game was still close, with the Broncos up 16–10. Denver needed another big play.

Malik Jackson (#97) scores a touchdown for Denver by landing on the fumble in the end zone.

As he knocked over Newton, Von snatched the ball out of the quarterback's hands.

Denver's defensive players sacked Cam Newton seven times during Super Bowl 50!

Super Bowl MVP

During a play in the fourth quarter, the Bronco's linebacker did it again. Von forced another fumble by Newton! This time, Denver's T.J. Ward **recovered** the ball. A few plays later, the Broncos scored again. Denver won 24–10!

Von was proud of the win and honored to be named the Super Bowl **MVP**. "It feels great," he said. "This is what you work for. I am so proud of my teammates."

Von celebrates after making a sack during the Super Bowl.

Von is only the fourth linebacker to win the Super Bowl MVP award.

Key Players

There were other key players on the Denver Broncos who helped win Super Bowl 50. Here are two of them.

Peyton Manning #18

- **Position:** Quarterback
- **Born:** 3/24/76 in New Orleans, LA
- **Height:** 6′ 5″ (2 m)
- **Weight:** 230 pounds (104 kg)
- **Key Plays:** Led the Broncos to four **field goals** and a touchdown; at age 39, became the oldest quarterback to lead a team to a championship

Brandon McManus #8

- **Position:** Kicker
- **Born:** 7/25/91 in Philadelphia, PA
- **Height:** 6′ 3″ (1.9 m)
- **Weight:** 201 pounds (91 kg)
- **Key Plays:** Made four field goals without a miss

Glossary

AFC Championship Game (AY-EF-SEE CHAM-pee-uhn-ship GAYM) a playoff game that decides which American Football Conference team will go to the Super Bowl against the winner of the NFC (National Football Conference) Championship Game

defense (DEE-fenss) players who have the job of stopping the other team from scoring

draft (DRAFT) the event in which NFL teams take turns selecting college athletes to play for them

end zone (END ZOHN) the area at either end of a football field where touchdowns are scored

field goals (FEELD GOHLZ) placekicks that go through the uprights, giving the kicking team three points

fumbles (FUHM-buhlz) balls dropped or lost by players

interception (in-tur-SEP-shun) a pass that is caught by a player on the defensive team

legendary (LEJ-uhn-dair-ee) very famous for something in the past

linebacker (LINE-bak-ur) a defensive player, on the second line of defenders, who makes tackles and defends passes

mentor (MEN-tawr) a person who acts as a teacher or guide to a younger person

MVP (EM-VEE-PEE) letters standing for Most Valuable Player, an award given to the best player in a game or in a season

NFL (EN-EF-EL) letters standing for the National Football League, which includes 32 teams

offense (AW-fenss) the part of a football team that does most of the scoring

playoffs (PLAY-awfss) a series of games played after the regular season ends to determine a champion

quarterback (KWOR-tur-bak) a key player on offense who makes passes and hands the ball to teammates

recovered (rih-KUHV-urd) gained possession of a ball after it was dropped or lost by the opposing team

rookie (RUK-ee) a player in his or her first season in a pro sport

sacks (SAKS) plays on which the quarterback is tackled behind the line of scrimmage

suspended (suh-SPEN-did) temporarily removed from a team for breaking rules

Bibliography

Bishop, Greg. "Wild Ride: Tale of Super Bowl 50 Champs Broncos." *Sports Illustrated.* (February 15, 2016).

Official Site of the Denver Broncos: www.denverbroncos.com

www.nfl.com

Read More

Howell, Brian. *Denver Broncos (Inside the NFL).* Edina, MN: ABDO (2011).

Scheff, Matt. *Superstars of the Denver Broncos (Pro Sports Superstars).* Mankato, MN: Amicus (2016).

Learn More Online

To learn more about Von Miller, the Denver Broncos, and the Super Bowl, visit www.bearportpublishing.com/SuperBowlSuperstars

Index

AFC Championship Game 16–17
awards 9, 10, 20–21
Brady, Tom 16–17
Carolina Panthers 4–5, 18
Chicago Bears 9
childhood 6–7
Dallas Cowboys 15, 17
Denver Broncos 4, 7, 10, 12, 14, 16–17, 18–19, 20, 22

draft 10
Gray, Cyrus 7
high school 6–7
Jackson, Malik 18
Jerod-Eddie, Tony 7
Manning, Peyton 22
McManus, Brandon 22
Moore, Damontre 7
New England Patriots 16–17

Newton, Cam 4–5, 18–19, 20
Pittsburgh Steelers 17
Seattle Seahawks 12
Super Bowl XLVIII (48) 12
Super Bowl 50 4–5, 18–19, 20–21, 22
Texas A&M 6, 8
Ward, T.J. 20
Ware, DeMarcus 14–15